The Floating World
Gabriela, Twelve Silken Buttons

A.A.Cain

Lunchtime Erotica by A.A.Cain

Copyright © A.A.Cain 2019

The Floating World – Gabriela, Twelve Silken Buttons
Lunchtime Erotica by A.A.Cain

Published by: A.A.Cain
PO Box 117, Campbelltown, South Australia, 5074

Email: writingbyaacain@gmail.com

Pocket Book Edition: 2019

ISBN:

print: 978-0-9876330-9-5

Contents

Epigraph

During the Tokugawa Period in Japan (1600 - 1868) the word *ukiyo* came to describe the meaningless pleasure and ennui that was the lifestyle for many people in the cities, particularly Edo, Kyoto, and Osaka. "Floating World" is the English translation.

It is said that the geisha, or courtesan, occupied a separate reality known as *karyukai*, or the "flower and willow world". The geisha entertained their customers with the tea ceremony, and with a cultured presentation of music, dance, and conversation.

Closing Day

"I'll take the counter this morning, if you like," said Gabriela, pulling her black hair back in a twist and flicking a band around the thick coil. She inspected her red lips in the mirror, stretching out her fingers to see the same colour red on her nails. Gabriela hoped he liked red. She'd bought the matching colours the night before, and found herself thinking of the tall, silver haired man who came into the café most mornings.

"Yes, that would be good," replied her boss, Ruth. She looked across at Gabriela and smiled, amused at the younger woman preening in the mirror. She reached over and adjusted Gabriela's collar, spreading the lapels wider to reveal a delightful spray of freckles on her upper chest. Like a lotus branch in a beautifully etched Japanese print, the spray descended into the divide of Gabriela's divine cleavage. "Just one button," warned Ruth, "discreet, but enticing enough for their morning eye." She made one final correction to Gabriela's collar. "Perfect."

Being a savvy business woman, Ruth knew the importance of attractive staff behind her counters. Little Amanda had been wonderful, but she and her boyfriend were travelling overseas, so Ruth was grooming Gabriela to take her place. She was pleased with the young woman's slightly exotic appearance, a touch of Asia perhaps, or maybe South America. Some ancestral trace gave Gabriela dark, dark eyes and a darkness on her skin.

There was also a touch of something else about Gabriela, some ethereal essence Ruth couldn't quite put her finger on. Something about the young woman was, well, different. Ruth had a bit of the witch about her as all women do, and the sight some call intuition, some call second; but Gabriela... Ruth couldn't grasp it, and that made her curious.

Ruth had seen Adam's eyes narrow the first time he saw Gabriela, a sharper focus, just as they did when Amanda enticed him with her morning smile. Ruth wondered how long it would be before Gabriela tried her own witchery on Adam, for he was the kind of man who paid attention to his women, and they wanted that. Ruth could see from the way he talked to her girls, and the way he laughed with the woman with the long blonde hair, that he gave each of them his undivided attention. Each moment, theirs alone.

Even Ruth, who was older and wiser than all her girls, even Ruth couldn't resist his smile. She'd caught herself playing with her hair... Being the boss, Ruth could place a touch of possession on his arm when he was in her café, but wasn't so sure of herself outside her own space. Ruth enjoyed Adam's under-stated confidence and liked his presence in the café, as did her girls. Ruth suspected he gathered attention in most rooms he walked into, in his quiet way.

"Good morning, Adam. Is it your usual this morning?" Gabriela smiled up at him, the corners of her eyes genuine. "It's a latte, isn't it?"

"Yes it is, Gabriela, yes it is. One day I'll surprise us both and order something different." Adam looked upon the girl and saw her lips. He passed her the change, brushing her fingers with his, and saw the colour of her nails. "But not today."

"Look, the right money. You always bring the right money." Gabriela rang up the sale, glancing behind him. There was no line. "Will you be coming back later?"

"Later today, do you mean?" Adam replied. "No, probably not." He saw a flash in her eyes, something quicker than thought. "Why do you ask?"

"Oh, I just wanted to make sure I said goodbye before I go. Today's my last day before the holidays, I'm not in tomorrow." Gabriela looked straight at Adam and took in a breath. The shadow between her breasts tightened.

"Thank you," he said, "that's lovely, that you wanted to say goodbye to me. Are you going anywhere over the break?"

"Yes, I'm going home for Christmas, Christmas with the family." Gabriela touched the buttons on the cuff of her sleeve, and Adam saw her fingers turn.

Adam smiled as he fully registered her nails matched the red of her lips. "Will you be back in the New Year, then?"

"Yes. The café is shut for the next two weeks, after tomorrow, but I'll be here when we re-open."

"Well, I'll see you then." Adam heard the door behind him open. "Can you wait?"

She laughed. "I'll have to, won't I?"

"Yes, you will!" Adam moved aside for the next customer. "Have a lovely holiday, Gabriela. I'll see you soon."

On the flight between cities Gabriela sat in an aisle seat, just in front of the wing. As the cabin attendant did the safety drill Gabriela found herself admiring the woman's firm thighs and taut ass. The attendant stood right beside Gabriela, her crotch at eye level. Her slacks were tight fitting, and Gabriela admired the little curve of belly descending into the V at the top of her long legs. Gabriela was so close to the woman, she could have undone the belt and slid her hand around...

Gabriela closed her eyes, resting her hands on her own belly, a little curvier than the cabin girl's. She dozed lightly, semi lucid, and found herself re-playing the conversation with Adam that morning, saying goodbye to him. Goodbye also meant a hello later, and Gabriela imagined the soft look on his face when he saw her again. As she shifted her head from one side of the headrest to the other in a sleepy turn, Gabriela's fingers caressed her belly. In her dozing mind, she saw Adam's hands take up a cup and she saw the curve of the cabin girl's ass. Something mingled and was made in her mind. Desire.

Gabriela drifted in and out of sleep during the flight, and by the time the plane landed, she had a whole conversation ready for when she next saw Adam. She wondered if he liked her, until she realised of course he did. That's lovely, that you wanted to say goodbye to me. His words echoed and gave her peace of mind. Gabriela stretched out her fingers in front of her, admiring her red finger nails. She momentarily wished her fingers were a little longer, then turned her hands over and forgot about it.

Gabriela stood and reached for her bag in the overhead locker.

"Here, let me help." The young man in the seat opposite was already standing, lifting his own bag down.

"Thank you, that's very kind." Gabriela smiled at him.

"No problems. Come on Dad, let's go."

Every son has a father, thought Gabriela; every daughter, too. The older man looked across at her and his eyes creased, a quick glance down to her lips and back to her eyes.

Gabriela's return smile was an automatic response, the fractional tilt of her head a sub-conscious recognition of his appreciation. She took her bag from the boy, and looked again at the man.

That's lovely. Adam's voice was in her head. Gabriela smiled at the thought of him. The boy's father thought the smile was for him, but it wasn't. Not today.

"Hello Dad, thanks for picking me up. Mum not with you?"

"No darling, you know what she gets like before Christmas. The kitchen's out of bounds and I just do as

I'm told. It's safer that way." Gabriela's father closed the car boot and turned to his daughter, his eyes soft at the sight of her. "How's my darling Gabs? It's been too long, honey, I've missed you."

Gabriela hugged her father close, her arms wrapped hard around his back, squeezing him tight. "Me too, Daddy, I know I should come back more often, but I'm always so busy." She tilted her head up and gave him a quick kiss on the lips, then buried her head in the crook of his shoulder; always her safest place, even when she was a little girl. "I'm home now, though. It's good to be back."

"You're by yourself again," her father said. "When..."

"Oh Daddy, don't. Not now. Mum is impossible, not you too."

Gabriela's father studied his daughter and didn't understand how this vibrant woman was always alone. As a girl at school she'd had the usual crushes, slammed doors and a repeated broken heart. He knew there were a number of disappointed boys, and later, sobbing girls writing bad poetry for her, and they were all good kids. Gabriela left a trail behind her, but kept walking. Had he brought her up to be too independent?

"It's OK, Daddy, don't fuss. I'm fine. I'm just not interested."

Gabriela's father knew his daughter well enough not to probe. He would take her side when her mother, as she inevitably would, took up arms against their daughter's single status. "Leave her be, Elizabeth, leave her be," he'd say. "She'll be fine, you'll see. She just hasn't met the right person yet."

Gabriela sometimes wondered about herself, but didn't fret. As a teenager she had put up with fumbles in the back seats of cars and movie theatres and later in bedrooms, given boys hand jobs and the occasional blow job, wiping cum from her hand. But whenever it came to her own pleasure, she found her partners to be too young, too inexperienced, and she kept putting away her virginity, saving it for another day, another man. She left her teens with it still intact and proceeded into her early twenties quite unfussed about its presence. She just hadn't met the right person yet.

She didn't dwell on it. She had prepared in her mind some words to calm her mother down, when the inevitable questions came. Gabriela's father, she knew, would be in her corner with his shoulder the perfect height for her to rest her head on, his arm around her back.

They chatted about this and that, and Gabriela remembered just how comfortable she was around her dad. She looked across at him, his concentration on the road ahead. Even though he was driving, she put her fingers to his cheek, grazing the stubble there. I love you, Dad, she thought. Her father looked across at his daughter beside him, his Gabs, and his heart melted as it always had, from when she was the tiniest thing, her eyes flashing with her stubbornness and passion for everything. He didn't need to say anything at all. Gabriela knew his love was always there for her, just her.

The next two days were chaos and Christmas; too much eaten on the day and eaten too late, presents placed under the tree and Gabriela's father playing Santa, ho ho ho, then Gabriela was exhausted. The end of the year caught up with her and she slept, long and dreamless, the heat flaying her naked body under the sheet.

When her father went in later to turn off her bedside light, he smiled when he saw Gabs' hand clutching her old faithful teddy.

"Elizabeth," he said to his wife, "it's just as well we kept all those old toys for the grand-kids..."

"But we've got no grandchildren," she complained, "Gabriela won't..."

"Hush," he replied, "don't." He was gentle, but wasn't prepared to let her start. "I was going to say, just as well we kept them. Gabs is in there, remember her old favourite Ted? She's clutching its paw in her hand." He paused. "She's gorgeous. Our twenty-five year old daughter, and she's still got her little teddy." Gabriela's father stopped and pondered. "Sometimes, she's still my little girl, then she's all grown up." He shook his head. "My little Gabs, my darling Gabriela."

The next day Gabriela slept late, her parents moving around the house as quietly as they could. In the afternoon, Felicity, her oldest, closest friend from her school days came over. They had known each other since they were fifteen, and Flick was always welcome in the house. Back then she was a permanent fixture, and now Gabriela's parents made a fuss whenever they saw her.

"Hi, Mr and Mrs G. It's been a while. I only see you when Gabs comes back home, which she does less and less now."

"I know. It's a shame really, but what can we do? Gabriela insists on living interstate. We wonder what she's hiding, sometimes."

"Mum, god, I'm not hiding anything! How many times do I have to tell you?"

"Tell us what, darling?"

"There isn't anybody. Grrr, how many times, Mum!" Gabriela gave her usual response and her mother eventually let it go.

In Gabriela's Room

Later, up in Gabriela's room, Flick asked, "is there anyone Gabs, who you're interested in, even remotely?"

"Even remotely?" Gabriela paused. "Well yes, there is. Sort of."

Felicity didn't say a word, and continued to plait Gabriela's hair into a thick braid.

"Kind of," said Gabriela, articulating something in words for the first time. She'd thought it, but had never actually said anything out loud to anyone. But she could tell Flick anything, everything. "But nothing's happened. We chat, when he comes into the café, but that's all."

Felicity waited. Her fingers pulling and teasing on Gabriela's hair, she loved the soft feel of it, and it brought her close to her dearest friend. Her fingers caressed the hair, and every now and then she brushed it to her lips. Gabriela's eyes were closed as she luxuriated in the deep massage of her scalp, and never saw.

"Have you said anything to him," Flick asked, curious. She knew Gabriela's history with men, how she passed them by.

"Not really. Sort of," Gabriela replied. "I did make sure he knew I wanted to say goodbye to him, before the holidays."

"Really? What did he say?"

Gabriela remembered every word. "He asked, can I wait?"

"Wait for what, Gabs? What will you have to wait for?"

"Do you know," pondered Gabriela, "when it comes down to it, I don't know what I'll have to wait for..."

"It sounds to me, Gabs, you might have a crush on this man. Is he worth it, do you think?"

Gabriela was silent. Her pause was so long and unusual that Felicity stopped braiding her hair, and the stillness in the room somehow shifted and twisted with revelation.

"I think," said Gabriela slowly, "you're right. He might be absolutely worth it. Worth everything."

Felicity's fingers started their movement again and she thought of ceremonies and sacrifices. "You will tell me, won't you?" she asked, "when something happens."

"When something happens? But nothing's happened."

"You'll have to wait then, won't you?" said Flick, tying Gabriela's hair off with a band.

The young women loved each other's company, it was as if Gabriela had never gone away. They'd laughed and cried together for a decade; surviving, as so many girlfriends didn't, those years immediately after school when friendships ruptured and lives moved on. They often pondered it, "did you hear about... did you know that... I always knew she was..." and came to the conclusion it was their differences that kept them together.

There was something else too, that began as teenage girl curiosity and became a regular ritual, sustaining them both, drawing them closer each time. A necessary thing.

"Promise, Felicity, we'll always do this, whatever happens. Even when we're sixty. Promise."

"Do women bleed, Gabriela? That's my promise."

It began simply, teenage girls comparing themselves, then young women discovering themselves, then adults enjoying themselves. "When we're sixty, it'll be a celebration."

It always began slowly.

Gabriela turned to Felicity and pulled her to her feet. Standing side by side in front of a floor length mirror, they compared their heights. At fifteen, Gabriela had been taller, but was slowly overtaken by Flick so now there were several inches difference in their heights. Flick was a slender woman, small breasted and long boned, athletic. Gabs was curvier, her waist small. She favoured long flowing skirts that swirled from her hips, her breasts shifting beautifully as she turned, brushing against Flick's arm.

"You do that every time," Flick commented. "You just have to do it, don't you?"

"Do what, darling? Oh, my lovely full breasts swaying in my bra, brushing against your arm. Do I make you jealous, lovely girl, with your perky tits all tight and firm, but oh so small?" Gabriela's eyes sparkled, she loved this teasing play. "God, you're a bitch. Look at you, twenty five and you still don't need a bra."

Gabriela's eyes darkened and she licked her lips. "Come here, honey, come here." Her voiced deepened, husky with anticipation. "Let me see you."

She reached her hands to the waist of the taller woman and eased the tee shirt from Flick's tight jeans. Slowly Gabriela pulled the cloth up Flick's body, trembling slightly as she did so. Her movement was slow and teasing, they were in no hurry. She licked her lips again, and tilted her head up to Felicity's mouth. Their lips touched, and Gabriela's hands stopped. Their kiss was gentle at first, tentative. They remembered their first kiss, when there was a sweet innocence between them. But then the hungrier older women soon took over and their tongues thrust deeper.

Flick sucked Gabriela's lush bottom lip into her mouth, nipping it with her small teeth, tasting the linger of the red lipstick Gabriela wore. "Strawberry lips, I can taste the blood of strawberries on your lips."

Hearing her words, Gabriela wanted nipples like berries between her teeth. She quickly pulled Felicity's tee over her head, revealing those high, tight tits with big full nipples, succulent. "God, Flick, let me," and she pushed the other woman down onto the bed, her mouth following hungrily those perfect nubs, sucking first one into her mouth then the other. Gabriela opened her mouth wide around Felicity's breasts, sucking in as much of each tight, hard tit as she could.

Flick moaned and her body twitched with the sharp pleasure. Her hands were frantic too, reaching for the buttons on Gabriela's blouse, trying to undo them quickly. "Too many buttons, Gabs, too many." Her fingers fumbled, but she pulled and tugged, and the blouse opened wide, revealing Gabriela's lush, dropping breasts, barely contained in her bra. "Oh, god I love your breasts, your big swaying breasts."

She reached for the open front of the blouse, pushing it back from Gabriela's arms to reveal all of her friend's deep cleavage and the lovely roundness of the belly below. "Ohhh, Gabs, let me." Felicity pulled the curvaceous woman down to her body, feeling those soft mounds against her tight nipples, the soft belly against her harder, tighter gut, but always soft lips, so sweet. Flick fought with Gabriela's blouse, pulling it down her arms, desperate to get it off.

Gabriela pushed herself away from her girlfriend's body, sitting up high, gripping Felicity's hips between her thighs. She bent back away from Felicity's groping hands, teasing her arousal, laughing as she batted those hands away. "Darling Flick, what's the matter, can't you reach me, my glorious tits?" She held both breasts in her hands, offering herself up to the other woman, delighted in the effect she was having on Felicity. "Do you want to see me, all wonderful and naked?" Her voice was a sing song, and she whispered, "do you want my lush nipples between your lips?"

"Fuck, Gabriela, you know I do. Show me, bitch, show me."

"Oh Felicity, that's no way to speak to your oldest, dearest friend, not a polite way at all. Bitch?" Her eyes sparkled, revelling in the helpless woman trapped between her thighs. "I'm not a bitch. Just for that, I'm not going to show you!" Gabriela reached behind her back, quickly unclipping her bra, then brought her hands up

17

under the cloth, hiding her breasts from Felicity's hungry eyes. She pressed hard against her own breasts, easing the ache developing behind her hard nipples.

"Gabriela, please, please let me see, please," Felicity pleaded, caressing the waist of the ripe body above her.

Gabriela leaned forward, taking her hands away from her breasts, and their weight swung them low over Felicity's head, just out of reach of her lips. She pulled the bra away from her arms and dropped it on the bed. Her full breasts swayed beneath her body. "Ahhh, Flick, here they are, all full and hot for you. My nipples, look, see how hard they are, just for you." She lowered herself some more, and Felicity suckled a tight nipple into her hot mouth, sucking and gently biting on the nub.

Gabriela moaned with delight and after some seconds, offered up her other breast for suck. "Oh yes, that's right, suck my breasts hard, oh, lovely girl. God, I love this, hmmmm."

For minutes they pressed their breasts against each other, taking turns to nip and suck and bite. Their first frantic undress slowed and they found themselves lying on their sides, their hands and fingers slow caresses. Gabriela held her beloved friend's face in her hands and gazed upon Felicity, soaking in her high cheeked beauty with her eyes. That was how their love started many years before, holding each other's young bodies, close and innocent, comparing themselves.

Felicity loved the heavy weight of Gabriela's breasts, and slid her fingers along her deep cleavage, twisting firm nipples between her finger and thumb, tracing the spray of freckles. Their movements slowed between them, leaving slow sensation and lingering touches.

"What are men's hands like, Flick? I don't know."

Gabriela wondered now, having left boys behind many years before and never finding a man who would take his time with her, a patient man. A longing was building up in her, a curiosity; some uncoiling thing to break down the small dread inside her, a vague fear time was passing by and leaving her behind.

Flick was the only woman she had known intimately, almost as well as she knew herself, but at least Gabriela knew the sexual pleasure a woman could bring. She couldn't remember the fumbling boys from her teens, but the idea of a man who knew how to seduce her, ah now, that was something different.

"A man's hands, Gabs?" Felicity pondered. "I don't know how to describe the difference, not really."

She looked at her own hands. "Bigger. Longer fingers. Sometimes gentle, sometimes not. I don't really know." Felicity thought back to their earlier conversation. "You might have to wait, Gabriela."

She was silent for a moment, then intuition hit her. "This man from the café, Gabs. Has he really noticed you, do you think?" Her own hands stopped moving on Gabriela's breasts. "What are his hands like?"

"Warm. Even on winter mornings, they're warm."

"I meant what they look like, long fingers or short, wide hands or what." Felicity laughed. "But you tell me you know they're warm already!"

19

Felicity moved her hands down Gabriela's belly to the waist of her skirt, sliding down the zip she found there, probing their way inside Gabriela's knickers. "I think Gabs," she lowered her voice, "I think you might need to make this man see more of you. That's what I think."

Gabriela shivered with the run of Felicity's fingers over her clit, partly from Flick's light touch and partly from the idea of Adam. Adam. His fingers trailing over her belly, like Felicity's? Could she imagine it?

"What should I do? I don't know what to do, not with a man."

"Oh Gabriela," Flick replied, "I think you'll do just fine, if he saw you with your gorgeous curves and your red lips." She undid the button on Gabriela's waist band and tapped her on the bottom. "Lift your bum, so I can get this off."

As she slid the skirt down Gabriela's legs, Felicity sat up and looked at the woman lying abandoned before her. Gabriela's throat was flushed red with her arousal, and the top of her chest too, the blush darkening the freckles between her breasts. Her nipples were dark brown nubs, hard and tight, standing up from smooth skin. Between her sprawling legs, the crotch of her panties was a spread of dark wetness.

"Gabs, a man, finally. Are you ready for a man?" Felicity's voice was high and playful, teasing, but she knew this was a serious matter. Her darling Gabriela, wanting a man now? "Who is this man, Gabs? Describe him for me." Reaching down to Gabriela's waist, Flick peeled the wet knickers down. "Oh fuck, the lucky bastard," she whispered, "he's going to have that. So wet."

Gabriela's sex was dark between her legs, a fine tangle of black hair coiled tight along her lips, a slick of wetness shining. Her sex was lush and opening, a butterfly of inner lips rising from the darker outer pair. Felicity looked, long and hungrily, then slowly spread the inner lips to reveal a darker red, almost purple. "The lucky man," she repeated, "a paradise awaits." She slowly ran her fingers into Gabriela's cunt, finding her rough spot and pressing there. "Make sure he finds this place," she said, as Gabriela arched her back in ecstasy.

Felicity eased her fingers from Gabriela's hot sex, knowing she'd tease Gabriela and return there. But not yet. There was more she wanted to know about Gabriela's mystery man.

"Nooo, don't go, that's so good." Gabriela clenched her thighs together to trap Flick's hand, but the other woman was relentless and pulled away.

Flick needed to know more about this man. She wasn't exactly jealous, but it was something close. "What's his name, Gabriela? Tell me his name."

They'd had long conversations like this before, slowly circling around the topic of discussion, interrupting themselves with a kiss or playful tickle, giggling and gasping between their sheets, until finally they were beyond words and the only sounds in the room were low moans and sighs. But this was serious. Gabriela had never spoken about a man like this before, and Felicity needed to know more about him. She needed to approve.

21

"Adam. Come back to me, Flick. Don't go." Gabriela didn't want to trade pleasure for information, but sometimes there was no pleasing Flick. "His name's Adam."

Flick's fingers grazed across Gabriela's clit as a reward, sliding pleasure up into her throbbing cunt, connecting the image of this man in Gabriela's mind with desire and lust, cunt proud and deep.

Felicity sensed a change in her friend. She wanted Gabriela to want a man, to be filled and full. She grazed her fingers down the long slide of Gabriela's wetness. "How old is he, Gabs?"

"How old? Oh, fuck, your fingers, they feel so good." Gabriela keened with pleasure and struggled for words. "He's... He's... Jesus Flick, you're wicked, stop... he's... I don't know, fifty." Her breath caught up, "older maybe, ohh."

"Fifty, Gabs?" Felicity's fingers continued their pressure, sliding the start of a slow fuck into Gabriela's clenching cunt, pushing the idea of cock into her. "He's old enough to be your father."

"I know. Is it wrong?" Gabriela bucked her hips up, clenching Flick's fingers inside her.

"Oh no, Gabs, every girl loves her Daddy, don't you think?" Felicity fucked two fingers deep into Gabriela's sliding cunt.

"He's not my father, Flick, he's... Adam, he's... Oh Flick, fuck, stop, you're teasing me." She moaned, and cried out his name. "Adam, he's..."

Felicity was satisfied. "Sshhhh, my darling, no more questions." She leaned down to Gabriela's mouth, her kiss and darting tongue a reward, and her fingers sliding around Gabriela's clitoris a promise. "Ssshh, lovely girl. Let me. I want to."

Felicity gazed down at Gabriela, her legs spread wide on the bed, her throat and chest flushed; and she loved her sweet friend so much, so very much. She ached inside, and nearly wept, but Gabriela's pleasure was all that mattered now. Felicity cared nothing for herself at this moment, Gabriela was her purpose and her prize.

And Adam's prize. Felicity didn't know this man, but trusted Gabriela in her choice of him. But who would seduce who? How would Adam know?

Gabriela looked up at Flick and saw something in the other woman's eyes, flickers of emotion running through her. She reached up her arms in a wide embrace. "Come to me, Flick. I'll tell you, I promise, but it's us now, just us. I love you, Flick, don't ever forget it. You're my first girl."

"But you've found a man, Gabs."

"Don't be jealous, Flick, he couldn't ever be like you." As was always the way with their deepest, most intimate conversations, conclusions were reached and promises made. Gabriela realised what her words meant. Adam was inevitable, and he didn't even know. Witches were at work, spells being woven like a tapestry, a cloak; spells sewn like the finest embroidery, a web, a veil.

"No, I'm not jealous. Envious maybe." Felicity paused. "Gabriela, did you know, back then, what saying no to all those boys meant?"

"No, I don't think so. They just weren't right for me, that's all I knew."

"Adam's right though, isn't he?" Flick thought of practicalities. "How will he know?"

"Tomorrow, Flick, we'll go buy me a dress. If I'm going to try to catch his attention I'll need a dress, a beautiful dress." She pictured herself. "A long flowing dress, tight at the waist."

With that thought in her head, Gabriela reached for the waist of Flick's tight jeans and undid the single button there. "Lift your bum," she said, "so I can peel these things off you. Too much talk, Flick. We always talk too much, don't we?"

They stopped talking, but the room wasn't silent for long.

Later, in the still of the night. Gabriela's father made his round of the house, like he always had since Gabs was tiny, checking the outside doors were locked and all the lights were off. He saw light under the door to Gabriela's room, and knocked gently. Hearing silence, he softly opened the door and went to the bedside table to turn the lamp off.

"Pull the covers up Daddy, I'm cold." Gabriela's sleepy voice was just a tiny whisper, her words automatic, triggered by his presence.

He looked down at the two women lying naked, back to back on the bed. He smiled as he gently covered them with the sheet, not wanting to wake them.

"G'night, Gabs," he whispered, "love you."

"Love you back, Daddy." Their night time words, always, but she was asleep, Flick too.

He left the room, quietly shutting the door behind him. He wouldn't say anything to Elizabeth, but wouldn't forget the sight of them, either.

The First Day Back

"Gabriela, hello. It's good to see you. Did you have a good break?"

Adam greeted the young woman warmly, remembering she had gone back to her family for Christmas.

"Yes, it was lovely to see Mum and Dad. I slept most of it, though."

"Lucky girl. But now back into it, yes?"

"Yes. A new year. New promises, new things." She smiled up at him. "But you, back here again? It's a latte still?"

"Yes, it's still a latte." He gave her the right money, and her fingers were warm. "I'm quite predictable, I'm afraid."

"But I always remember your order though, that's useful."

"I guess it is, useful."

As he turned from the counter, he noticed Gabriela touch the buttons on her cuff, and thought it a familiar gesture, but couldn't quite place it. Then he remembered. Before the holidays, when she said goodbye to him, she had made the same gesture. It seemed almost a nervous thing.

As he waited for the barista to brew the coffee, he admired Gabriela from behind. She was efficient, her hands busy with the till and change, but she was hidden behind another counter, so he could see only her profile, the fall of her hair, her back. And the ridge of the bra across her back. Idly, he wondered if her bra was red, to match her lips. He smiled to himself. How would he ever find out?

The barista called Adam's name, and he took the coffee. As he turned outside the door, he glanced back. Gabriela watched him leave, her fingers twisting the buttons at her cuffs. Adam saw the movement and wondered if it was a subconscious thing. Her smile was for him, and he took it with him down the street.

Gabriela followed him with her eyes, and as she did so she reached inside her collar and adjusted the strap of her bra. She was aware of the weight of her breasts and the ache behind her nipples, and the shift of her flesh felt good. It was a conscious thing, because of him. Her bra was a pale shade of blue, a nice contrast to her dark skin.

That night, Gabriela rang Flick. "I don't know what to do. I've seen Adam, but how do I get him to see me outside the café? How do I say something?"

"You need to get him somewhere where he can see you in the dress. Once he sees you in the dress, he'll be interested." Felicity paused, and the line hissed with distance. "What time do you get off work? Could you get away an hour or so earlier on a Friday? Meet him somewhere?"

"I guess. I can ask Ruth. Tell her I've got a doctor's appointment or something."

"That would work. Meet him a couple of blocks away from your work. Somehow suggest drinks."

Gabriela could tell from Felicity's staccato speech she was thinking as she was talking.

"A drink. What's a good celebration?" The logic of Felicity's thinking caught up with her. "A doctor's appointment won't work." The line went quiet. "You just need to be a damsel in distress. That always works in books."

"It's not a book, Flick. That won't work." Gabriela was disheartened. "Grrr. How can I make him see me, outside work?"

"What time does he finish? Bump into him as he walks past."

"What? No, surely that won't work. It's too obvious."

"It works in books, Gabriela, so you can make it work."

"The way you're talking, I need a library." There was a long silence. "Are you there, Flick?"

"Yes. Too much thinking, Gabs, we're thinking too much."

"What do you mean?"

"Simple is best. Just give him your phone number, Gabs. On a piece of paper. Easy." Felicity laughed. "Who's not going to call you? If a woman gives a man her phone number, of course he's going to call."

Adam unfolded the piece of paper, smoothing it out in his palm. Her name, Gabriela, was written in a looped, feminine hand, together with her number.

"Adam," she'd said, her voice low and her eyes looking down. "Please, I'd like you to call me. I've..."

He remembered her earlier words and the nervous movement of her fingers around the cuffs of her blouse. He'd taken the tightly folded paper quickly between his fingers, and touched it to his lips. The movement pulled her eyes to his face, and he mouthed the words, I will, saving her from her own fear and fuelling his own curiosity.

He wondered at her action, and felt she was brave doing it, or terrified. Perhaps both. He didn't know what she wanted, but thought she must want it keenly. The next steps, wherever they might lead, were now his to make it easier for her.

"Gabriela, hello. It's Adam. You wanted me to call. Is it a good time?"

"Yes. Adam. It's me. I..." She didn't know what to say next. "Can I..."

"Gabriela, how about I pick you up somewhere, and take you somewhere else? You can ask me then, when you're not rushed." Adam took control. "When can you be ready? And where?"

There was a silence on the line for a moment, then Adam heard an intake of breath, and she gave him her address, and a time. "Is that time OK? Does it suit you?" Now that Gabriela had made up her mind, clocks were ticking and time was everywhere.

Adam was slower, more patient. In his world, time always slowed and spiralled inwards towards a moment. He was intrigued, no doubt: what did the young woman want? Did she come bearing gifts or seeking offerings? He instinctively thought of a still place, a quiet place, where she could slow herself down. The image of fingers twisting and turning on the cuffs of her blouse caught in his head and he wondered about that.

In the Garden

He walked to the step of her door, a small town-house on the south side, with a tiny walled garden. Frangipani blossom brushed his sleeve and he was scented by the flowers. Adam was aware of a heat low in his groin and his senses tightened. His vision sharpened, and he breathed in deeply the sweet scent of the flowers. He heard movement on the other side of the door, and stepped back.

Gabriela opened the door and Adam saw her silhouette framed there, the small curve of her waist the perfect width for his hands if they danced, but they weren't dancing yet. He reached out his hand to escort her over her own threshold, and she rested her fingers on his. Adam raised her hand to his lips, and it was the perfect gesture.

"Nobody's ever done that before," she said, "it's my first time for that."

"Gabriela," he replied, "it won't be the last."

He turned and she followed, pulling the door shut with a solid clunk. Her past closed behind her.

"Come, I know a lovely place." Adam gave her his arm, and escorted her to the car, her dress flowing with movement. "Your dress, it's beautiful." Gabriela's eyes shone, she must tell Flick everything he said.

"Thank you," she said, "this is the first time I've worn it."

"It's a special occasion then." Adam looked down at her, "And I'm the lucky man to be seen with you." He opened the passenger door, admiring her legs as she swung them into the car. He reached for the seat belt, for the pillar was a long way back, and passed it to her. He watched as Gabriela took the buckle in her hand and clicked it in place, and he saw two buttons on the cuff. Her wrist was delicate. Her hair was coiled high on her head in a twist, escaping strands soft and dark against her throat.

Adam took in a breath and began to see all of her, assembling a collection of glances into a complete vision of a woman. He moved around the front of the car, so she could see him.

"Have you been to the Japanese Garden, Gabriela, on the edge of the park lands?"

"No, but I've heard about it."

"It's a quiet place. It'll suit you." Adam started the car. "It's exotic and slightly mysterious." He glanced across at her and wanted to reach out and touch her cheek, to prove she was real. But he didn't, afraid she might vanish, not real.

"Am I?" she echoed, "exotic and slightly mysterious?" She looked across at him, and wanted to touch his cheek, but he wasn't her father so she couldn't. "I've never been called that before."

"Another first then. So many firsts, Gabriela." He slowed, and turned onto a road running beside the parkland, trees in the distance and hills beyond. "I'm beginning to think I'm your first man." He glanced at her, and saw the sudden twist of her hands in her lap.

Gabriela, startled by his words, took in a deep breath and felt a sharp stab deep within her breasts. Her nipples felt huge, as if every nerve pulsed there, and she knew if she pressed her hand to her flesh, her nipples would be hard, hot hard. She felt heat in the base of her belly, and her sex bloomed and opened. Her senses felt visceral and raw, and she saw veins threaded on the back of Adam's hand. A tiny pulse beat there, beating blue.

And so they awoke to each other's presence. Gabriela knew instantly her choice was right; and Adam sensed he was chosen, but he knew not for what.

Adam brought the car to a stop, and they turned to each other.

"Hello, Gabriela, finally. You're here now."

"Yes, Adam. I am. I'm here, with you. I like it."

"Come then, my lovely, let's go to the garden and we can walk. Then we can sit and talk." He gazed into her eyes. "You can tell me what it is I can do for you."

He knows, Gabriela thought, he knows I want him, but he can't know for what.

She's chosen me for something, wondered Adam, but what?

The Garden was a gift from a sister city, and was a small, self contained enclosure separated from the bare grass paddocks by hedges and high fences. Water surrounded an island that could be reached by flat stone bridges.

Circuitous paths meandered through exquisite vistas, cleverly designed and contemplative, each turn perfectly constructed for the view beyond. It was well established, with tall pines casting shade and keeping the walks cool.

Other than Adam and Gabriela, it was deserted. A gentle breeze blew warm against their skin, and Gabriela's dress swirled and lifted as she walked. They went side by side silently for a while. Adam, who knew the garden, set a slow pace; and every now and then Gabriela would stop as they turned a corner and saw a new miniature landscape, a rock for a mountain, a tree for a forest.

"It's so clever how it's laid out. Each stopping place has a perfect view." She looked up at Adam, and leaned into his arm; the pressure not quite the weight of her head against his shoulder, but almost. "It's quiet, isn't it? The sound of the little waterfalls, it's just gorgeous."

She stepped away to look at him, this tall man in a quiet place, and wondered how he saw her.

The flow of her dress as Gabriela stood before him was like a veil of water falling. It was pale and cream, a contrast to her darker skin. The skirt of it flared over her hips and clinched into a tight waist, and the bodice hugged her full breasts pushed high. Adam counted eight buttons down the front, from high on her chest to just below the base of her belly, and two buttons on each cuff. Adam remembered her words, it's the first time I've worn it. The dress, then, was chosen especially for him.

Twelve silken buttons, and each to undo.

"Your dress, Gabriela, is beautiful. You're beautiful." Adam loved the brightness in her eyes and her smile as she heard his words. "Let's sit, that bench is shaded and cool."

The bench was under a timbered pergola, offering visitors a view of a raked gravel sea with islands of rock placed in a precise pattern, lichens and moss a tiny microcosm. Adam and Gabriela sat beside the sea. Tiny birds, wrens, substituted for seagulls and were tame, flitting to their feet then gone when no seed was dropped. Gabriela laughed at their quick, darting flight.

"Look, there's the male, bright blue." She touched Adam's arm, pointing. "See, on the branch."

Adam saw, but the young woman beside him interested him more. He said nothing, not knowing what she wanted. He knew this peaceful place would calm Gabriela, and when she was ready, she would find her words.

Gabriela wandered at first, telling him a little of home, a little of her work. Adam learned about Felicity, "My closest friend, she knows me so well," and saw the love in Gabriela's eyes for her.

"Will I meet her, your friend?"

"Oh maybe, one day. She knows about you..." Gabriela stopped, realising she had said too much. "I mean... I've mentioned you. One of my customers..." She stopped again, and looked at Adam for help. "Sorry, I'm..."

"Chattering?" Adam's voice was soft, gentle. He looked at the young woman beside him in her perfect dress, her hands gripped together in her lap to stop their movement. A sudden flash of instinct made him turn towards her, a quarter turn, and with one arm around her shoulder and a hand on her hair, he gently tilted her head so it rested in the crook of his shoulder, safe. "It's OK, lovely. Rest your head here. I've got you."

Gabriela sighed, tension spilling from her, and she relaxed against him. Slowly, she turned her head up towards his, her lips opening to just show her teeth. Adam looked down and saw her open mouth, her closed eyes, a faint flush on the side of her long throat. His lips touched hers, soft at first, then their tongues touched.

Gabriela's hand went to the back of Adam's head, pulling them together, and their kiss was long and sweet. Hungry but slow, their tastes mingled. Adam grew hard, and Gabriela was wet for him, but she wanted it to take forever, slowly and forever.

But first, Adam had to know. Gabriela pulled back and looked up at this man, this man who surely would know what to do. "Adam," she swallowed, and found some words. "Adam, this will sound strange, but..." Her hand touched the back of his hand on her shoulder for comfort. "I want... I need to tell you something. About me. You need to know something about me."

"What is it Gabriela, what do I need to know about you?" He caressed her hair slowly, calming her like a cat, waiting for her revelation. "It can't be bad, I wouldn't believe that." He kissed her again, to encourage her thoughts. "I'm sure I can cope." Adam smiled, but his blue eyes narrowed just a little, tell me.

Gabriela took in a deep breath, pressing her palm against his hand on her shoulder for strength. Adam stopped stroking her hair, and she knew she had to go on, to bring the comfort back, to get it done.

"This dress, Adam, It was Flick's idea. I..." She stopped. "No, I'm being silly. It doesn't matter."

"Doesn't matter, Gabriela? Are you sure?"

"Yes, I'm sure. It doesn't matter."

Gabriela changed the subject. "It's nice being here with you though, I'm glad you bought me here. It's peaceful."

Adam looked at her, having watched a myriad of emotions pass across her face. She said it didn't matter, whatever it was, but he could see that it was important. No matter, he was a patient man, he could wait. He would find out sooner or later, it was just a matter of time. Adam had plenty of that, and was used to a slow pursuit. It made a seduction more satisfying, the longer it took.

Adam gazed upon her still beauty, sitting there in her beautiful dress, and decided yes, he would put his mind to this woman. She was different to other women he had known, some essence in her wasn't the same. He was intrigued by her, and that made her interesting.

"May I, Gabriela?" Adam took one of her hands in his, and undid one button. His lips whisper kissed her wrist, and a tiny pulse heated the scent she had dabbed there earlier. Her scent rose, and Adam breathed it in deep. Her wrist was everything, it was the first moment of Gabriela's seduction, the first place.

In a Japanese garden, a thread of moments began, silken threads twisting around tightly; twelve silk buttons to be undone...

"Good god, Flick, his gentleness with me, I couldn't believe a kiss on the inside of my wrist could be so exquisite. Adam kissed my wrist, his lips like a butterfly quivering. That's all he did, Flick, there in the garden. I felt like those pictures of a hundred years ago, where the women flirt behind a fan and drop a handkerchief. He was so gentle, so delicate."

"What did he do next Gabs? What did he do?" Felicity wanted to know everything, every word, every tiny gesture. She couldn't wait.

"Goodness, Flick, you're so impatient!" Gabriela paused, teasing her darling girl, knowing what happened next and re-living it as she retold the moment. "Adam's so wicked, Flick. He knew exactly what to do."

"What, Gabs, what?"

"He undid another button, Flick, two buttons now. Both cuffs."

"Gabriela, you tart, you're shameless. Two!" Felicity could imagine the gorgeous smile on Gabriela's face, she could hear the joy in her friend's voice. "Oh, Gabs, can I have him when you're finished? I've never been undressed slowly, never. I'm so jealous." Felicity was worldly and knew men, but she'd never known a man like this man. "Oh Gabs, where did you find him?"

"In Ruth's café. In the mornings, just like that. Amanda served him first, and I could see how, when he spoke to her, nobody else existed. Then I served him for a week in a row. And he was the same with me. He'd talk to me, and all I wanted was for him to look at me again and again. It was only ever a minute or two, but I'd melt each time. I felt like a silly swooning school girl, but all I wanted was his smile. Just for me."

"And you wore red lipstick and matching nails. Gabriela, you're a total slut. You've started your witchy ways on him." Felicity was impressed. "How could he resist you?"

I couldn't resist you either, thought Felicity. Fuck, I'm jealous, she thought twice.

"When are you seeing him next, Gabs?"

I'm going to torture myself if he seduces her slowly, Felicity thought, thrice. And another witching woman awoke, and tendrils moved through the ether towards Adam, weaving a spell slowly.

Adam shivered, a ghost walking over his grave. He looked up, but no-one was there. It was a familiar touch, from long ago and tomorrow. He shook his head, clearing his thoughts.

His mind turned to Gabriela, and Adam pondered his next step. A long, slow approach might be best, tantalising and teasing, moving ever closer to the prize that was Gabriela, so many delightful stops along the way. He thought of those brilliant Japanese woodcuts from the nineteenth century, where seduction was hinted at behind closed screens, shadows and rain and blossoms falling.

Then Adam thought of another type of Japanese woodcut, where the sex was huge and joyous, with massive cocks and big hairy cunts, a maid stealing a glance from behind a screen, and luxurious cloth. Ah, so much inspiration.

And Gabriela herself, there was something divine and beatific about the young woman that entranced Adam, which made him adore her. He wanted so much to be held in her arms like some fallen angel, his own darkness purged by her grace, held safe. She wasn't the same as other women he had known, there seemed a different gentleness about her, some inner peace. He craved for it, to be held by her.

A Black Velvet Choker

"Gabriela, come, stand before me."

Adam gazed upon her as she stood before him, her hair long and dark and falling down over her breast, nearly to her waist. Her dress, as before, had swayed and swirled as she walked beside him, her heels clicking on the pavement. Now the flow of cloth was still, but the bodice swelled high with her breath.

From a pocket of his coat, Adam produced a black velvet box, and turned it towards her. Gabriela undid the small clasp, and lifted the lid.

"It's beautiful. Thank you."

"It's the first thing I'll place against your skin, Gabriela, and the last thing I shall take off. With it on, you'll stand nude before me; with it off, you'll stand naked." Adam moved towards her, lifting her face to his in a kiss. "If you'll let me, that is."

She stood still before him; and his fingers moved to the highest silken button on her bodice, undoing the button and revealing her throat. He swept the long weight of her hair into his hand, and coiled it up high and away from her neck. "Hold it up," he said, "and look at me."

Gabriela held her head tilted proud, and bared her throat to receive his gift. Adam took the black velvet choker from the box and undid its catch. He placed it around her throat and it was a narrow band of darkness against her dusky skin. He claimed her with it, and his promise of dropping it away from her skin was a sign of his confidence Gabriela didn't debate.

"Come, Gabriela, sit with me."

Gabriela sat beside him, and the buttons on her sleeves were undone, her wrists bare and slender. Adam took one hand in his, kissing the tips of her fingers one by one, then eased them, two at a time, into his mouth. His mouth was hot and her fingers heated. A nerve ran from each of her nipples to the base of her clit, and all three nerve centres peaked and tightened. Gabriela sighed, and fell against his chest, a hand against Adam's heart.

They kissed for a long moment, their tongues exploring each others' mouths. Gabriela crept sideways onto Adam's lap, half on and half off, and she felt his shaft hard against her thigh. She pressed herself against it, and was rewarded with a small intake of his breath. She pressed again, and took a tight tip of Adam's tongue into her mouth.

Gabriela closed her lips against the thrust of his tongue, and for the first time Adam forced her. She softened against his will and was not taken. She gave herself up, wanting him, her first time resisting him then letting the man in. Adam savoured the moment, and held her body against his.

Still curled on his lap, Gabriela touched the cuffs of Adam's shirt and undid the buttons, each cuff at a time. She said nothing, no permission sought, no permission given. Adam stretched out his arms to make it easier for her fingers, and she rolled each cuff up one turn. Gabriela took his fingers to her mouth and repeated the same tip suck that he gave her, and felt the length of his cock shift. She looked up at him, her eyes bright but less of a smile, concentrating on learning the length and angles of his fingers.

She splayed her hand against his broad palm, and her hand was smaller. She'd thought she wanted longer fingers, but his curled over the top of hers and interlaced, so it didn't matter. Their palms touched and were warm, and Adam placed his other hand over the back of hers and her hand was safe between his. Gabriela's free hand reached up to Adam's cheek and cradled his face. She watched his eyes close and felt an ever so slight change in the weight on her palm; and Gabriela knew some small tension in him was given up to her, that he too could soften and relax and sleep in her hands.

They were wordless, tiny flickerings of trust moving back and forth as their fingers made trails over skin and cloth and each other. Gabriela's eyes never closed, she took him all in, learning every small scar and line on his skin, learning a man.

Adam knew more, and was looking for something else, so his touch was different, less tentative. He undid two more of the silken buttons on the front of Gabriela's dress, and his fingers moved upon the upper curves of her full breasts, finding the divide of her cleavage and the long line to her throat. She was still curled on his lap so his exploration was uneven. Gabriela wriggled, wanting all of her skin to be touched, she was becoming hungrier now.

Adam gently turned, and lowered Gabriela to the couch so she lay there, her throat flushed, her mouth slightly open, oh for her sighs. He took a step back and stood upright and she lay before him, the long flow of the dress covering her legs, hiding her hips. Adam stood quite still for a moment, studying Gabriela, savouring her beauty, her quiet presence.

Gabriela's gaze on him was steady, she didn't look away, her eyes were black. Her eyes narrowed, so subtle he nearly missed it. A slight prickle went up the back of his neck, and what he thought was the want of her became a need for her. The air in the room shifted, and Adam felt a slight spin of vertigo. He tensed his legs, pushing down to the floor to steady himself, to catch his balance. Could she save him?

"Tell me, tell me, Gabriela, what happened next?" Felicity held the phone close to her ear, Gabriela's voice fading and falling with the distance, a faint echo doubling their voices, voices.

"He just looked at me, Flick, and it was like some strange light switched in his eyes. God, the way he looked at me." Gabriela's voice dropped to a whisper, as she remembered the moment. "The intensity of his gaze, I didn't know what it meant." She paused. "I just reached for him, I reached up to take him in my arms." Talking about it brought an explanation she'd not seen before.

"He seemed lost, Flick, so lost. I just wanted to hold him in my arms. So I did, Flick, I opened my arms to him and he came to me, and lay his head on my breast. Before, he'd held my hand in his, but now it was my turn to hold his hand between mine. His head on my breast, like a baby."

"What happened next, Gabs?" Flick whispered into her phone, not really believing what Gabriela was saying, but aching to hear every moment of it. She did not know Adam, but was astonished to hear of this intensity in the man, this vulnerability, and Gabriela's natural reaction. "Did you just hold him forever, Gabs? This man of yours?" Felicity ached for a man like him, who needed a woman so much. She'd never found one.

"Not forever, but a long time. I think he almost slept on my chest. Then he stirred." Gabriela stopped talking, and Felicity could imagine the look on her face as she remembered. "Oh God, Flick, his care for me, I couldn't believe how gentle he was with me."

Adam hadn't slept. He'd listened to the quieting hush of Gabriela's heartbeat as it calmed to a steady beat. Her breath was even and slow, and she matched the slow caress of his hair, her hand over the curve of his skull, to her breathing. He felt a natural stillness in the woman, so at peace with herself that she calmed him, soothed him.

Gabriela was a resting place for Adam. There were times in his life when he met a woman unexpectedly, when he wasn't expecting anything or seeking anyone; when a woman simply arrived in his life. He might be drinking coffee, reading a paper, and would look up at a sound, a movement, even a shadow; and there she would be, a newcomer in his life. Inevitably, he would be seduced by the magic the woman wrapped around him until he was helpless like Merlin trapped in Nimue's tree, until she grew bored and set him free.

This time though, Gabriela sold him the coffee and cleared away the paper after he had gone, and he was the newcomer coming into her territory, her café. Perhaps it was a reversal of the roles this time, where he cast the shadow, where it was his movement through the door that made her look up, that turned the moment around. Was he simply arriving in her life? He'd not thought of it like that before. Was he Merlin unbound, this time?

There was a mystery to Gabriela he couldn't place, a hesitation in her and something tentative. Several times now Adam had seen her fingers twisting around her wrists in a nervous motion, repeated and repeated. But she knew when it was right to beckon him into her arms and simply hold him, and he wanted to be held by her.

Adam lay with his head on her chest, his cheek pillowed inside her shoulder. He could see the faint beat of a pulse on her throat and if he listened closely, her heartbeat by his ear. Adam pushed a curl of hair away from her neck and felt an intake of breath. He stroked his fingers gently against her throat and heard a faint sigh, and the tiny pulse on her skin quickened. Ah yes, Adam thought, her heart beats a little faster for me.

Gabriela's fingers gripped part of her dress, and her eyes fluttered closed. Her hand stopped moving through Adam's hair, and there was a second reversal in the room.

Adam pushed himself up onto his elbows and looked down at the woman below him. Gabriela's eyes were closed, long lashes black, the colour in her skin rising. Her red lipped mouth was slightly open, her lips full and inviting. Adam kissed her softly, and her hand left the folds of her dress to find his, but his hand was gone.

Adam reached for a button on Gabriela's dress, two buttons undone down the front and now a third. The tops of her breasts were showing, the delightful spray of freckles descending into the shadow of her cleavage. The cut of the dress was deceptive, hiding the fullness of her breasts. With the buttons undoing, undone, her curves were full and enticing.

He passed a single finger down into the cleft, following the freckles but losing count, and was rewarded by a shiver of goose-bumps and another sigh, louder this time. Gabriela licked her lips, just the tip of her tongue, and Adam rewarded her with another kiss.

"Gabriela, we should eat. If I undo another button, we'll never make the restaurant on time." Adam got to his feet, and reached for her hands to pull her up. She swayed, and gripped his arm. "It's OK, I've got you."

He held her close for a moment, pulling her body to his and enjoying the press of his cock against her. He stepped back, placing both hands on her waist which was small. Gabriela delighted him, and Adam's eyes were blue, a smile in his eyes for her. She was real before him, not a dream. Adam adjusted the spread of her collar, pushing back the cloth to show her perfect cleavage. Gabriela smiled to herself and Adam saw it.

"Tell me. Am I amusing you?"

"No," replied Gabriela, "not at all. I was just thinking of Ruth's instructions."

"Ruth's instructions?"

"Yes. Just one button, she'd say. To entice them in the morning."

Gabriela saw herself in the mirror, and put her hand to her chest, spreading her fingers over the length of the buttons undone. "Three buttons, Adam. What would she think?"

"Clever woman, Ruth," Adam replied. "One for the morning, two by lunchtime, three buttons for dinner." He kissed her lips again, and wanted her.

Gabriela listened to the logic of his words, and knew there were five more buttons on this dress. Her breasts ached and her nipples were hard, and there were only three silken buttons undone on the bodice.

In the base of her belly Gabriela's wetness was full and ready, but he still didn't know she didn't know men. He was undoing her buttons one by one. She knew it was a seduction now, and she didn't know what to do.

"What did you do, Gabs?"

"I was tormented, is what I was, teased. I loved it."

Felicity lay back on her bed in her sweats. She'd just come in from a run when her phone rang and it was Gabriela, so she went straight to her room, dragging her runners and socks from her feet as she did so.

"He lay on my shoulder for I don't know, ten minutes, fifteen, I can't really say. Then it was just like another switch went click in his head. He didn't say a word, just started stroking my throat. God, Flick..."

Felicity lay there, picturing Gabriela with this man, wishing it was herself in their room. She was hot from her run, and peeled her top from her torso to reveal a simple tight sports bra, lines of sweat curved under her shallow breasts. Flick brushed her fingers through her short hair, pushing it away from her face.

"... my skin shivered with goose bumps when Adam ran his finger down my cleavage..."

"Wait, Gabs, how many buttons? Cleavage? How much cleavage?"

Flick was beyond curious, she wanted to know everything. It wasn't fair, here she was, fairly experienced with boys and men; and her sessions were clothes off, jump into bed, quick fuck, usually OK and sometimes she came. And there was Gabs who didn't have a clue, being romanced and charmed, seduced properly by someone who...fuck, someone she wanted. Someone who knew what he was doing. Felicity gripped the phone closer with one hand.

"Three buttons. I even measured the length of them with my fingers spread. But he's not even seen my bra yet, Flick. He's so polite, reaching down to pull me up from the couch, holding me steady." Gabriela paused, remembering. "Not so polite, really." She giggled.

"What Gabs? Why not polite, really?"

"Because when he held me close, I could feel him against my thigh." Gabriela paused, waiting for Flick's response.

"Against your thigh? That's a pretty close hug, Gabs."

"Not just a close hug, Flick, that's not what I meant."

"What are you ta...?" Felicity finally got it. "Jesus, Gabs, what the fuck, he's hard for you?"

"Don't sound so surprised, Flick. I can be pretty hot too, you know."

Gabriela flicked her hair back, and even though Flick was a thousand miles away, she knew exactly what look was on Gabs' face.

"Sorry baby, I know you can." Felicity was quick to calm her friend before she took off like a colt. Fuck, I'm so jealous, she thought.

Flick looked down at herself, and her nipples were hard and long, pushing up points through her bra. Her breasts ached, and between her legs her sex wettened and she knew what was going to happen next.

"Tell me, Gabs, what happened next?" Her voice was low, with a huskiness from her growing arousal.

Felicity peeled the bra over her head, and looked down to her long nipples, like the tips of her little finger, hard and tight. She cupped one palm over a breast and pushed hard to stop the ache. Her sex bloomed and she sighed.

"Was that you, Flick?" Gabriela's voice softened. She knew it was.

"Adam got my long grey coat from behind the door, and draped it over my shoulders. 'To keep you warm,

52

Gabriela,' he said. He always calls me Gabriela. It's so sophisticated when he says it. Gabriela."

She paused, letting her friend picture them both together. "Then he escorted me to his car. Properly escorted me, Flick, opened the car door and everything, handed me the seat belt even."

Felicity twisted a nipple between a finger and a thumb, and pulled it tight, pinching a small pain into her breast. Oh h, that felt good. More. "Where did you go, Gabs? Tell me." Torment me, because it's not me, going in the car. "Wait."

Gabriela heard movement, and the single squeak of a bed spring, and she knew Flick was shifting on the bed, lifting her bum, no doubt, to pull her bottoms and knickers down. Gabs and Flick, they knew each other so well.

Gabriela pictured Flick's strong, toned belly, and the hard curve of muscle at the base of her gut, diving into plain cotton-tails, her sexy knicks, as Felicity called them. Down now, kicked off from the ankle, her long legs spreading wide, one knee bent, cooling her cunt to the air. Her long smooth sex was neater than Gabriela's little crinkled butterfly wings, her lips smooth and fine, a high clit exposed.

"We just went to a restaurant, Flick. A beautiful one, perfect food, we shared a bottle of wine. Adam knew the chef, who came out and made a fuss."

"What did he do, Gabs?" Felicity moaned, as she spread her lips and slid her fingers inside. "Tell me."

"We chatted, this and that. He listened to me." Gabriela was thoughtful. "He probably indulged me, let me go on about myself too much. And you, Flick, I told him some more about you."

Flick's fingers stopped sliding between her sex lips. "What did you tell him about me, Gabs?" Her fingers penetrated, and she started a slow fuck into herself, wet and slow. The idea of this man, even filtered and made fanciful through Gabriela's narrative, was penetrating deep into her mind, and she wanted him. Her fingers pushed.

"I told him we'd known each other since we were teenagers at school."

Felicity lay the phone on her pillow, and rolled onto her front. She raise her ass high, placing her weight on her knees, long, lean thighs spread apart. "What else, what else did you tell him about me?"

"I described you to him."

Felicity's fingers spread aside her lips and she wet her fingers, sliding them around and over the nub of her clit. Pleasure started to cycle deep into her body. She pressed her breasts down onto the sheets, the friction grazing her nipples, tightening them. "Tell me, Gabs, talk to me. Tell me about Adam."

"In the restaurant, Flick, or later?" Gabriela teased her darling, who couldn't keep the springs quiet any more.

"Oh h Gabs. Later? You lucky bitch, fuck. Not fair, I want him too." Felicity would soon knock the phone onto the floor, and faintly hear Gabriela's giggle, then her whisper.

"Come, my darling, make yourself come. I'll stay with you while you do. Naughty Felicity, playing with herself while I talk to you on the phone."

Gabriela told Flick what happened next, her voice low and husky with the memory of it. With her phone on the floor, Gabriela's voice was small and distant. Felicity came, nearly sobbing with her own pleasure, but not quite.

After dinner, where Gabriela had charmed the chef and wondered whether Adam thought the waitress delectable, they drove down to the sea. The low surf was moonlit and phosphorescent, the night sky sprinkled dark with distance. A gentle breeze blew the swirl of Gabriela's dress against her legs and she spun around twice, to show Adam the movement of the skirt. She was luminescent, her long hair midnight black and falling long to her waist.

"The moonlight, Adam, your hair is silver in the moonlight." She took his arm, and they were a couple by the sea, en promenade.

"The flow of your dress, Gabriela, it reminds me of a poem. 'Like a skein of loose silk against a wall.' The woman in the poem is not like you though, she's bored and wants an indiscretion." Adam looked down at the young woman on his arm. "You're not bored."

Gabriela glanced up at him. "No, not at all bored, Adam, not when I'm with you."

"Is this an indiscretion, do you think, you having dinner with me? I'm twice your age. More than." Adam was curious for her response. The confidence revealed in the phone number written in her looping cursive impressed him; but the nervous twisting hands, they intrigued him too. She was two contradictory women, almost, in one lovely package.

"More than twice my age. Yes, you are, but so what?" Gabriela looked straight at him, and her eyes were black, jet black. "All it means is I'm half your age. I don't have a problem with that." She interrogated him. "Do you?"

"No, I don't. Some people might though."

"Oh goodness, who cares? You're not my father, that's the kind of silly thing he worries about." She paused. "Actually, Dad's not so bad. Mum's the nightmare, she's always on at me. 'Gabriela, when are you going to bring a nice young man home?' she'll say. And my answer is always the same. 'I've not met anybody yet, Mum.'" She looked at Adam, thoughtfully. "I wonder what she'd think of you?"

"Gabriela, I'm not a nice young man," Adam replied. "And I'm not sure I'm ready to meet your mother." He laughed. "Is she like you, Gabriela?"

"Stop it. You're teasing. You mustn't. We've only had dinner, and you've taken me to the Japanese Gardens. That's all." She was defending her mother and justifying herself, and knew it wasn't all, not one bit. God, Flick, she thought, I've got three buttons undone on my dress and my sleeves are a lost cause, and I have a velvet choker around my throat; and Adam's talking about my mother. Help, what I do?

"What were you like as a young man, Adam?" She changed the subject, and it was a genuine interest. She tried to picture him at her age, but couldn't. She took his arm again, and leaned her head against his shoulder, steering him back to the car. A cool breeze had sprung up, and she shivered.

"Gabriela, are you getting cold? I shouldn't have brought you here, that was thoughtless of me." Adam placed his arm around her shoulder, draping her with his coat. And it was natural that she placed her arm around his waist and they had a perfect pace together. "There, darling, are you warmer now?"

Gabriela thought of her father, that was exactly the kind of thing he would have said. Would you approve of Adam, Daddy? she thought, and vaguely thought he might. She smiled to herself, and this time Adam didn't see it.

She remembered the boys who courted her at school. "You look after my girl now, she's the only one we've got." Her dad was only half joking when he said it, and the lads were bright enough to know that. "Yes sir, Mr G, I will." Gabriela was always home by eleven, and her dad would pop his head in her door. "How'd it go, Gabs?" Sometimes she would tell him, patting the bed cover for him to sit beside her, her eyes bright with the tell of it. And Gabriela's father learned that his daughter was strong willed with a mind of her own, and unreachable standards all of her own.

"What were you like when you were young?" she repeated. Gabriela was more interested to discover what his young women were like, but didn't know how to lead that question. She thought he might come around to them, his own moments and tells.

"A young man, Gabriela? I don't know if I can remember back that far. It's a long time ago."

"You're not Methuselah or Noah, Adam, even if you do have a biblical name." She wasn't going to let him get away without an answer. "It's not that long ago. You can tell me."

Even in the dark, Adam knew her lashes fluttered up at him and her eyes were innocent and huge. She hugged his arm, to let him know she was playing, and he loved her confidence in teasing him. They were nearly at the car, and he turned to her and placed both hands on her waist. Gabriela wanted to place her hands on his upper arms to feel his strength, but didn't. She left her arms loose by her sides.

"When I was young, Gabriela, someone taught me to do this."

Adam pulled her to him, one hand circling around her waist, the other moving confidently to her back, between her shoulder blades. And he pulled her to him, tilting her head to his. "Taught me this, Gabriela," and he kissed her, long and passionate, holding her close, oh so close.

Gabriela's hands came away from her sides, and one was around his neck, the other on the back of his head, pulling his mouth to hers, pulling him to her, don't let go, don't let go.

She broke the kiss. "Who was she, Adam? What happened?"

"She left me, Gabriela, that's what happened."

My god, thought Gabriela, didn't she know what she was doing, this woman? She reached her hand to his cheek, and felt a tiny weight as Adam rested his head on her palm, like a pillow. Oh, Adam.

"Adam, can we go now? I want to go."

Their moods had changed, like switches suddenly do, and Gabriela wanted him so much. She didn't know what to do, and her heart pounded. Her breasts ached and her nipples were like jewels, hard and firm, and her cunt bloomed. She could picture Adam's head on her shoulder, and that had to be enough, she didn't know any more. Five buttons, Flick, but I don't know what to do.

"Sweet Jesus, Gabriela," moaned Flick, her fingers wet within herself, "what did you do?"

The Last Button

Adam took her back to his apartment. It was on the tenth floor of a small high rise, its display windows looking over the park lands, with a distant view to the eastern hills and a glimpse of the bay to the west.

On the way there they were both silent in the car, the shifted mood from the sea and Adam's lost loves hovering over them like ghosts. Gabriela understood this man was carved and bound by the women in his past, and she understood too her innocence ill equipped her for competing with them. She resolved then, that she could only be herself, and that would have to be enough. She could be no more.

Her fingers toyed with the velvet band around her neck, and the movement of her red-tipped fingers was slow. Gabriela was no longer nervous; she walked in the footsteps of his teachers and she did not think he would have known frail and fragile women. Her hand rested on his thigh, a cat's paw quietness, no weight at all.

As they walked from the basement car park to the lift her small hand found his, and they said not a word. Adam knew, even if she did not, her touch was a lifeline. He was still formal with her, ushering her through his door with his hand in the small of her back, then taking her coat from her shoulders like a cloak.

"A drink, Gabriela, what will you have?"

Adam showed her the lounge room, and she stood absorbing the view while he clattered cupboards and clinked glasses in the kitchen.

"Here, my lovely," and Adam stood by her, slightly behind, his tall presence solid in the room. Gabriela rested her head against his shoulder and felt safe. His hand rested gently on Gabriela's waist, just beside the curve of her hip.

Adam placed his glass on a table and moved behind her, his hands cupping the small swell of her belly. Gabriela was astonished by the silent intimacy of this touch, and grateful for his gentleness. She was realising this man was full of care and devotion, so careful towards her, and slow.

The rest of her body was burning with a hot heat, her sex was molten and smouldering for him, and her high breasts hard and tight, her nipples full. Yet this man held her softest swell, her centre, with respectful hands, gentle hands. She didn't know a man could be so gentle.

Or so certain. Adam lifted a hand from Gabriela's belly and slowly unlooped the fourth button on the front of her dress, exposing the full creamy curves of her breasts and the laced tops of her bra cups. Gabriela gasped, and her breasts swelled high. He didn't say a word, but cupped her belly then slid his other hand inside the cut of her dress and cupped a full breast. He trapped her there, in his hands, and even if Gabriela wanted to, she could not have escaped.

She leaned her head back towards his and turned her face up, seeking a kiss. Oh sweet god, Adam, you hold me so close. How do you know what to do?

Oh, my sweet Angel, you turn your lips to mine and your eyes never let me go. Sweet Jesus, is this how love begins? Not again, not now.

"Oh fuck, Gabs, I can't bear it." Felicity clamped her thighs tight on her hand, two fingers deep inside herself in a solitary fuck, her other hand squeezing her breast oh so hard. She ached, but couldn't ease it.

Adam held Gabriela, a full breast in the palm of one hand and the swell of her belly soft in the palm of the other. They were motionless like that for a long moment, then her fingers came up to the fifth silken button on her dress, and she undid it. The undoing revealed both her breasts high, the whole embroidered lace of her bra and its silken cups. Gabriela held the back of Adam's hand and pressed it to her heart.

"Adam, I need to tell you something." It can't wait, not now, not any more.

"Is it important, Gabriela?" He held her close, his hands warm and his body standing firm behind her. "Of course, it must be important, or you wouldn't be telling me."

He let her go, and turned her towards him, smoothly pulling the sides of her dress together so she was unrevealed. Gabriela held the unbuttoned dress together with one hand, pulling it up close to her throat. She held his gaze. He held both his hands to her waist and looked upon her. She placed her hand on one of his, taking confidence from the touch of him.

"I... you're my first, Adam, you'll be my first man." She didn't look away. "If you continue to undress me, that is." Undress me, Adam, I want you to.

Adam's hands remained motionless about her, and the moment turned in on itself.

Her heart beat faster and she took another breath, a double intake that was almost a sob, but not quite.

"I..." Adam stopped. Ahh, I see. Me? "You've never... Me, you want me to be the first man you sleep with?"

"Yes. No. I don't know. Yes."

Gabriela, normally so sure of herself, was no longer sure at all. Could she trust this man, trust him fully and deeply enough to give him her greatest gift? Between her legs her cunt opened and bloomed and wetness slipped, and she ached to give him herself. The gift of her trust, her complete and unconditional trust. To feel a man within herself, finally, fully and completely and hers, all hers.

Gabriela wanted this. Her cunt wettened and the base of her belly tightened, and a long ache began. Gabriela's fingers turned and were nervous at her wrist, playing with the cuff on her sleeve. She held the folds of her dress together, hiding her breasts as she revealed her truth.

Adam gazed at her, his mind shifting quickly through the imponderables of her request, at the enormity of her gift, the responsibility.

"Why me?" She had reduced him to fundamental questions.

"Why you? Why you, Adam? Don't you know?" Gabriela looked at him, more certain now. "It's you, Adam, because I trust you. You'll never let me fall. You're too kind for that." She held his eyes, refusing to let her gaze drop, and reached her hand up to his cheek.

Adam tilted his head to rest it against the tiny pillow of her palm and could sleep there.

"Silly boys and young men, Adam, they could never catch me if I fell." Gabriela believed in him. "You'll always keep me safe."

Adam lifted his hands from her waist to her face, and cradled her cheeks like a prayer. He held her for a moment then fell into the blackness of her eyes. She closed her eyes, trapping the vision of him in her mind, and now her world was touch. Gabriela gave herself up to him completely, and didn't need light to see.

Adam gently took her hand from her throat, and she let go of the cloth. Her hands dropped by her sides, and she stood before him.

Slowly, and without a word, Adam undid the remaining three buttons of her dress, three silken buttons and they were all undone. He took one step back from her, and slid the dress back from her shoulders. It fell to the floor with the softest sigh of silk, and she stood before him, her head high, proud. Her eyes were closed, but she knew Adam gazed upon her, his eyes revelling in her revelation.

Gabriela stood before him in simple lingerie, delicate and tasteful, soft against her skin, lightly embroidered. The garments were a paleness against her tanned skin, hiding and revealing every curve. Black stockings on her legs, black straps to a plain garter around her waist.

"Your shoes, you don't need them any more." Adam's voice was low.

Gabriela stepped from her heels, and they fell inside the puddle of her dress. She stood delicate before him, her hands by her sides, her long hair falling.

"Gabriela, you're beautiful. Let me look at you."

She let him see, but kept her own eyes closed. Too much.

"Wait." Gabriela heard a quiet slide of fingers on cloth, and felt the movement of air and a drop of cloth. She guessed Adam had pulled his shirt from his body and dropped it to the floor. She stood before him, still.

And felt him close. With a deft touch, Adam reached behind Gabriela and took the strap of her bra between his fingers, unclipping it from her back. She felt the whimsy cloth drop away, the straps sliding from her shoulders, and the weight of her breasts were heavy on her chest. They were pressed against him, her hot flesh against the heat of him.

Adam's hands curved around her back, and he held her naked torso to his. Gabriela placed her hands softly against his back, and if he was an angel, would have felt wings. She nuzzled her lips to the base of his throat, tasting his skin. Adam's hands lifted through the silken smoothness of her hair and he cradled the back of her head.

"Gabriela," he whispered, "it's me, I'm here."

"You are, Adam, here with me." They were simple vows, and the truth of the moment.

For Gabriela, seconds ticked by and the moment grew longer and longer and it was all there, everything forever. Her heart beat was uncounted, always ever.

Adam's time spiralled in on itself and his time stopped, nothing, no more, never. He needed to hear Gabriela's heart, to be alive.

"Wait," he said, "just a moment."

Gabriela opened her eyes to see him go from the room, his naked back and broad shoulders. She knew his shape from his suits in the morning, and liked what she saw. She looked down upon herself and saw her full breasts, tipped hard with dark nipples, darker brown against her dark skin, and liked what she saw. Gabriela covered both breasts with her arms, suddenly shy, not yet used to nakedness with anybody but Felicity.

Adam must have known, for he returned with a long embroidered gown and draped it around her back, hiding her luscious curves. The cool cloth felt wonderful on her skin, soft and smooth.

"Thank you, Adam. It's a beautiful gown." She turned on her toes, a small pirouette to show him and to hide herself.

"Japanese, it's late nineteenth century. But I'm not sure where from, or who would have worn it, back then."

Gabriela wrapped herself in it and was coy. But coyness was no match for Adam's confidence, for he simply knelt before her, split the drape of the gown from Gabriela's thighs and unclipped the garter straps from the tops of her stockings. He then peeled the knickers from her hips and slipped them down her legs. Still kneeling, he pressed his cheek to her small swelling belly, and held himself there, one arm stretched up her back, under the cloth of the gown.

The triangle of dark hair was soft to the touch of his palm as he cupped the mound of her Venus, his fingers splayed upwards to her navel. Gabriela still stood with her legs together, but she could feel the heat of her cunt blaze within her.

Adam stood, and wrapped the gown around her. "Don't get cold," he said. "Stay warm." I can wait, he thought, she'll open the gown when she's ready.

I'm not quite ready yet, thought Gabriela. But how can I still be dressed when he's just undressed me? How many veils will he strip from my skin before he sees me?

"Come, Gabriela, come through to my room."

"Oh fuuck," keened Flick, as Gabriela told her the tell. "Fuck, Gabs, will you tell me what happened? Don't you bloody dare hang up. You've got me dripping here, listen." And she held the phone down near her sex and Gabriela could hear the slick and wet slide of Flick's fingers.

"But Flick, he's barely touched me at this stage." Gabriela teased her friend, and was wet herself as she remembered.

Adam pulled back the covers on his bed, and split wide the curtains so moonlight poured into the room. The apartment was on the tenth floor, impossible to overlook, high above the streets so nobody else mattered and the world was far away.

Gabriela watched as Adam disappeared into the bathroom where she heard a run of water and some quiet movement. Despite her inevitable countdown towards moments she could only imagine, Gabriela was calm within herself. Her pulse was fast but steady, and with her cuffs gone and silken buttons undone, there was nothing left to hold onto in twists and turns. So she settled like a cat settles, curled and calm.

She heard the light switch click, and she looked up as Adam came into the room naked, walked to the window and stood there. He said nothing and let Gabriela see him. She looked, and saw the silvery grey hair on his head, his long limbs still slender, and his ass not quite so tight as once it might have been, but still shapely.

"Turn around, Adam, I want to see you walk towards me."

He did so, and Gabriela saw fine silvery hair on his chest, going darker down onto his gut. She saw the thick hang of his cock long against his thigh and liked the shape of him. Adam was full but not hard, the head of his cock still partly covered by his foreskin. A line of darker hair ran from his navel down around the base of his cock and over the swell of his balls. As he walked towards the bed, his cock swung and began to thicken at the promise of her.

"Adam, come to me." Gabriela held her arms out wide to him, inviting him to her body and would cradle his head to her heart. Her nipples were thick and hard, and her sex wet, so wet.

She turned ever so slightly on the bed with one arm outstretched on the sheet, and Adam lay beside her, his body covering half of hers. He kissed her with the softest kiss and tasted her lips, then ran his mouth, a warm breath, down the side of her throat. Adam lay his head on her shoulder and heard her heartbeat and was held by her.

He had all the time in the night with Gabriela, and over his years he had learned slowness and patience. Adam thought she would give herself to him in her own time and in her own way, and he wondered what moods might wash over her as her arousal heightened. He knew from her stories of Felicity that Gabriela knew her pleasure and how to find it, but now she would be discovering a man, learning his pleasure too, and how to share it. Ah woman, he thought, we will be wonderful together.

"Gabriela," he whispered, just to hear her name.

"What is it, Adam?" Her voice was low. She rested her hand on his shoulder and his skin was surprisingly soft.

"Oh, I just like the sound of your name. Gabriela." He looked up to her face and touched her cheek with his fingers, lightly, a delicate touch.

She smiled down at him, her eyes bright and alive. She took his fingers in hers and touched them to her lips. "Gabriela," she said her own name for him and it was her second gift.

They lay still for a minute or two, no longer caring about time for there was plenty of it. Adam began a slow, languid discovery of Gabriela's body, lingering his fingers over the curve of her shoulder, down into the long scoop of her waist, curving his palm over the swell of her hips and over her ass. His movements were slow, his hands stopping every now and then to caress another curve. Gabriela's skin prickled with goose bumps and he made his slow circuits a little heavier, shivering sensation into her.

Gabriela moaned with the pleasure of him, low in her throat, and her fingers began a different caress, more tentative, exploratory. She found sensitive places just inside his hip where her touch made him shiver, and she remembered them, learning Adam's delicate places. They shifted together on the bed, and Gabriela's legs slowly parted and his fingers found her.

Their hands continued curious wanderings, and slowly they rearranged themselves on the bed. Adam's cheek rested on her thigh, his face inches from her sex, glistening beads of wetness on her lips shimmering under the silvering moonlight.

Oh sweet goodness, Adam slid his fingers into her, and her hands stopped still. He tasted her, and offered up his fingers to her mouth so she could taste herself.

Gabriela's lick of his fingers was wet and warm, and she sucked the fingers into her mouth and made them hot and slick with her own saliva. She slid her own fingers into her cunt dark place, exposing the nub of her clit to his eyes, showing Adam how she stroked herself, sliding two fingers around the thickness of her clitoris.

Shimmering, shuddering, she touched herself and Adam gazed on her, concentrating on her fingers in herself, learning how she slid fast and circled slow. Her leg twitched, and he pressed his hand onto the back of hers and made her slow and stop.

"There's so much time, Gabriela, don't rush."

"I want all of you now, Adam, I'm greedy for you." Gabriela took her cunt wet fingers from her centre and, finding his long shaft by her face, slid a shining line with her finger along the length of him, and over the head of his cock. Fascinated, she chased after the shaft as it bounced from her touch, curling her fingers around it to hold him still. "Adam, your cock, it's so hot, feel the heat of you." She was amazed, finding for the first time so much heat.

Gabriela slid the circle of her fingers down the shaft, and over the head of it. "So soft, the head. Adam, it's incredible. I didn't know a man's skin could be so soft."

Adam closed his eyes with the pleasure of her slow discovery of his cock, and denied himself the wonder in her eyes as she touched him.

Gabriela was tentative with her touch, so delicate. She didn't yet know that she could grip him hard as well as stroke him soft. She curved the palm of her hand over the end of his cock, and he shuddered with the near pain of it. Gabriela saw his reaction, and stilled her grip, two hands now.

"Don't stop, ahh, that's good."

Gabriela tightened her hold on his shaft, and stroked slowly, firmer movements now, and was rewarded by a throb of his cock. "Oh, I see," she whispered, and touched Adam like she touched her own clitoris. "It's like me, only thicker and long." She measured the length of him with her thumb and fingers spread wide, and her hand was too small to know all his length.

She pressed her palm against Adam's side. "On your back," her low voice a command but he wouldn't say no. She rearranged herself on the bed, with her head resting on Adam's chest for a pillow, facing his cock which was the centre of her study now. She needed to know the length of him, his thickness that would be hers, the colour but he was silver in the moonlight, the softness of his skin which was hot velvet and smooth. Gabriela learned the cooler fragile weight of Adam's balls and they were big in the cup of her hands.

She tasted the length of his shaft with her tongue, and she kissed his cock sideways and left a kiss of her lipstick on him that was black in the moonlight, red in the morning when the sun rose; but the birds were asleep and there would be a cleansing place soon.

Adam coiled her long hair in his hand and breathed in its smell and felt its softness on his face, and he was filled with the sensation of her, this young woman discovering him in her new way. "Gabriela," he whispered, and she paused to hear his words but only heard his silence and his faster breath.

"I'm Gabriela," she whispered back, an affirmation of who she was and why she was here. She moved a little, opening her mouth around him for the first time, and took the plum of his cock head onto her tongue.

Gabriela slowed, to remember the stretch of her lips and the heat, the hard heat in her mouth. Her saliva flowed and the heat rose. Gabriela sucked on his head and made him moan. She did it again, and he moaned again. His hand gripped her hair and his body twitched.

Gabriela smiled to herself and released him. "There's so much time, Adam, don't rush." She trapped him once more, and her hands were slow on his shaft and her tongue twisted and curled.

Adam began a long stroke of Gabriela's back, down into the tight valley of her waist and over her rounded ass, along her thighs, turning his hand back up her spine. He found the long tightness between her thighs, and with each long sweep of his hand he teased fingers between her legs and she opened to him wider, until again his fingers found her wet centre and her musky scent, stronger now, was dusk and darkness in the air.

My turn, he thought, to taste her deep into my mouth, to drink her juice. "On your back, Gabriela, it's your turn."

She released his cock and obeyed, would never not. Her eyes were wide to the wonder of him, and they kissed but Adam was gone and her legs fell wide and her eyes closed. Adam knelt on the floor beside the bed, and took her thighs up in his arms, spreading her wide. She opened to him and wanted it all.

Adam placed the warm palm of his hand over Gabriela's sex, cupping the centre of her wet heat. With his other hand he reached up her body and felt the weight of a breast, rolling a hard nipple between his finger and thumb. For a long moment he held her sexual centres, joining them together through his own body and channelling his own energy around her.

He lifted his hand from her sex, and covered her with his open mouth, tasting her honeyed sweetness with his lips. Gabriela gasped at the heat from his mouth. Her hand pressed his to her breast. Adam probed the wet lips with his tongue and it was a little fuck. He swirled his tongue up and around her clit, licking her risen nub, sucking her hot centre into his mouth. Gabriela bucked up against his mouth, and was eaten by him. "Ahhh, more," she sighed, "yes."

Adam licked and probed, alternating between circles around her clit, then a firm tongue over the head of it, then descending to lose himself in the depths of her cunt. Gabriela moaned for him, "Mmmm, oh yes, there," and he settled to the perfect rhythm, pulling her sex to his mouth until it was all there was, a hot mouthing fuck into her. Slowly he licked Gabriela up to a first throbbing peak, then released her and did it again, surging sensation into her heat, her aching sex, and she came. Pushing her body down onto his mouth, Gabriela came, and a minute later came again.

Adam's ebb and flow against her cunt was relentless, until she came once more and pushed his face away from her sex. "Stop, it's too much." Gabriela cupped her own hand over her centre, pressing and pressing as she descended from the height of her pleasure, falling away from the strength of him and his control over her. "Oh sweet man, my god, look what you do to me."

Gabriela lay sprawled on the bed, her legs spread wide and her sex lips were dark and swollen, her juice glistening in the moonlight. Adam stood up from the floor and lowered his weight onto her, his long cock a burning heat on the flesh of her belly. Adam kissed the taste of her onto her mouth, and she sucked on his ripe lips, tasting herself and mingling his taste.

Gabriela wrapped her arms around his back, not letting him go, pulling his weight down onto her breasts, holding him, holding him. "I'm not letting you go, Adam, you sweet man. How do you know?"

"How do I know what, Gabriela?"

"How to make me helpless, a wreck." She kissed him, hard. "More."

"Fuck, Gabs, I'm dripping here. I'm so wet my sheets are wet, sweet Jesus."

"Oh Flick, maybe I'd better end the call, so's you can get some sleep." Gabriela teased her friend, knowing the last thing she wanted was sleep, and knowing the first thing Felicity wanted was Adam, or a man like Adam.

"Don't you bloody dare hang up." Flick was in agony and ecstasy listening to Gabs tell of her seduction and the sex, sultry and slow.

"More."

Adam gave Gabriela more. He had no choice, he was enraptured by this virgin woman, trapped by her, spellbound. He was no longer Merlin unbound, he was seduced, bound by her, trapped in her tree.

Adam lifted his weight from Gabriela and slowly moved back down over her body, his lips butterfly kisses on her neck and down over the small curve of her shoulder. He took her hand in his and reminded Gabriela where each of her silken buttons were.

"Two on each wrist, Gabriela, and the first ones undone in a Japanese garden." He kissed her wrist and saw a tiny pulse beat there, the smallest heart under her skin.

"Yes, and another two there. I was so daring, wasn't I?" She smiled at her memory, and the fall of leaves in a garden would forever remind her of him, and his silence there.

"Wicked, Gabriela, so bad."

"And Ruth's buttons, making me a temptress, show me where they were, Adam."

"Here." At the base of her neck, a kiss, just below the black velvet choker which was the last garment of her nudity for him.

"And here." Another kiss, on the slope of her chest, where the blaze of her freckles began. Gabriela's skin shivered, and her nipples tightened.

"And here, Gabriela," and he touched his lips to the crease of her cleavage where the spray of sun kissed freckles ended. Her sex bloomed, and where she was wet before, Gabriela wettened once more, her whole belly an empty ache, full of longing.

Adam suckled her tight nipples, one at a time, and Gabriela offered each breast up to him in her hands, then soothed the tightness with her hands pressed hard.

"The last buttons, Adam," Gabriela whispered, "before my dress dropped away. Where were they?"

Adam didn't speak, but showed her, trailing his tongue down the centre of her body towards her navel. He kissed her there, and her belly rose with an intake of breath, a gasping sigh. He kissed her again, where the finest thread of darkness furred a tiny seam on her skin, a dark trail moving down.

"Then what did you do Adam?" Gabriela's voice was the softest whisper, almost to herself, as she remembered her moments forever. "Oh god, yes."

Again, Adam took her sex into his mouth, his hot heat surrounding her sex, and their lips joined in a kiss, her sex lips swollen and dark. Adam tasted her, she was liquorice and honey with a delicate tang.

Adam made sure she was wet, so wet, then placed himself between her legs. Taking his cock in his hand, he carefully placed the head of it between her sex lips and held himself there, waiting for Gabriela to be ready.

Adam held his weight above her, gazed into the blackness of her eyes, and began to fall.

Gabriela knew exactly where he was, this man who waited for her, and she lay still beneath him. Still, so still, and she felt her heartbeat pulsing deep within her.

"Yes," she whispered to herself, and gave herself to him, this man she had waited for.

Adam gave himself up to her. As he slid slowly into her tightness, so slowly, Gabriela undid the clasp of the choker around her neck, so when she reached to his mouth for a kiss, a welcoming kiss, the velvet band fell from her throat and she was free and naked for him.

As Adam sank his length into Gabriela's sex, she struggled to keep her eyes open, gazing up into his. Adam paused, holding himself still within her, and Gabriela's eyes widened. Finally, as another inch slid inside her and she began to shudder with the pleasure of their joining, her eyes closed. Her throat and chest were flushed a deep red and Adam sank further, slow small thrusts, until his whole length was in her, flesh against flesh, heat within heat.

Gabriela whimpered, small wordless sounds in her throat, ohh, ohh, and she had him deep inside her body. Yes, mine, she thought and took him in. Adam felt huge inside her, and her whole sensation shifted to her cunt, her clit. Adam moved within her. Gabriela opened her legs wider, raising her thighs to his hips, taken, utterly taken.

Oh sweet love, Adam moved within her, long thrusts and slow. With the greatest care, with the greatest tenderness, he placed his arms under her knees and pushed them back with her thighs wide and high. Gabriela was spread, open, taking him in, and trusting Adam implicitly to love her love her love her as he slid his beautiful cock into her in slow, delicious thrusts.

Ohh, she sighed. Adam was so gentle, too gentle, her heart ached with his softness as he shafted her with his long cock, finally piercing the aching dam that had been building up all evening, all the long days, a deep swelling flow of heat and spreading sensation from deep inside her belly.

Gabriela opened herself for him, and he was in her, deep, one arm wrapped under her neck now, cradling her head to his, her cheek against his cheek, his lips soft kisses on hers. Oh yes, she sighed, love me, fuck me, my beautiful man, take me, take me. Make me yours.

She opened her eyes and held his gaze as he shafted into her, long and thick into the depths of her body, heat and sweat and a faster movement now, her pleasure a hot keen of ecstasy as she peaked in colours and white light, her body throbbing and shuddering under him as she came, her first orgasm with a cock inside her.

And her second, moments later, a long slow moment, wet and hard, pulsating around him. Gabriela thrust up to meet Adam, clenching his thick long shaft, rhythmic squeezes of her cunt like a hand. Gabriela's mouth was hungry for his, sucking in his tongue, eating his lips, fucking her tongue up into his mouth as he fucked her deep open cunt, faster now and Gabriela was helpless, helpless as he surged into her.

Adam felt a long deep heat at the base of his spine as his cum thickened and surged until with long thrusts, two and three pumps, his cum jetted hard as his back arched above her, creaming cum pulsed into Gabriela. The spill peaked her once more, "Yes," she cried, "oh h, ye es!" Her cries rang out in the room, a sudden scream silenced.

"I'm coming," Adam echoed her cry, "ahh h," and they surged and fucked and came together, high heat and white light and their eyes seeing nothing, and they came, clutching and holding and never letting go, they came together.

Gabriela clung to him and pulled his weight down onto her body, feeling his solidity covering her fragility. She shuddered with aftershocks rippling through her, long waves of pleasure taking her breath, gasping breaths nearly sobs but laughing too. Her glow began, that long warm place where heat became warmth, swift movements turned to slow caresses, and she fell silent.

Still inside her, Adam rolled on to his side and wrapped his arms around Gabriela, and hugged her to his chest. Safe, so safe. She smiled up at him and touched his cheek and he was there. Hers, this man, this lovely man.

They murmured to each other, low whispers and soft laughter, as they descended from the soaring heights of their orgasms. Their fingers traced spirals and patterns on each other's skin, and they became still in the night. At some point Adam shifted and his softened cock eased from her. Gabriela rolled away from him, their juice left a shining trail on her hip.

She nestled her ass back against Adam's groin and felt his heat there. She smiled, marvelling at the softness where once there had been hardness. Gabriela drifted into sleep, Adam's hand warm on her belly, cupping the small mound of it. Later, he too slept, and she was warm and small as he spooned her.

Several hours later Gabriela stirred, a chill on her skin from the cooler night air. "Pull the covers up, Daddy, I'm cold," she whispered, still asleep, not knowing where she was, who she was with.

In the morning Gabriela woke before Adam. She crept from the bed and went to the bathroom. After she flushed, she looked at herself in the mirror carefully, tilting her head first one way then the other. I'm no different, she thought, not really. She contemplated herself once more, looking at herself in the mirror, quite still, a serious look on her face.

She decided. Gabriela put her hair up in a twisted coil, and snapped a band about it. She took every ring off her fingers, her studs and diamonds from her ears, and gazed upon herself, utterly naked.

Proudly, Gabriela walked back to the bedroom. She went to the bed, pulled back the covers, and lay her head on Adam's chest. She gently placed a hand on his soft, sleeping cock and held it there, not moving.

In time, Adam grew hard and Gabriela held him, still not moving. When he finally stirred, waking slowly, she let his shaft go. She rolled on to her front, then kneeled, raising her lush ass high and placing her weight on her elbows. Gabriela's full breasts swung below her body, and she presented herself for Adam's morning pleasure. She took him very deep into her body - he was already deep in her soul.

"I don't get it, Gabs," pondered Felicity later that week. "Why did you take off the choker and all of your jewellery?"

"Because I wanted to be utterly naked for him, totally exposed and open for him; me, unadorned." Gabriela paused. "I trust him absolutely, Flick, but he doesn't own me." She took the long blackness of her hair in one hand and let it fall over her forearm and through her fingers.

"I'll go to him again, of course I will." She remembered everything. "How could I not?"

She wanted him and she'd give herself, gladly, as a gift, but he held no claim over her, none at all.

About the Author

A.A. Cain is an author of erotic tales living somewhere in suburban Australia. His work has been described as, "almost poetic; stories told by a crackling fire on a cold winter night, with a smooth whiskey in hand, listeners curled at your feet."

Cain's stories move from the floating world of city cafés and fashionable galleries, with contemporary men and women finding pleasure in familiar places, through to mysterious, mythical worlds populated with angels and astronauts, mermaids and men, and always, dark, seductive women.

.